KIT'S HILL

The Brief Chronicles
Book One

Jean Stubbs

SAPERE
BOOKS

KIT'S HILL

Published by Sapere Books.

20 Windermere Drive, Leeds, England, LS17 7UZ,
United Kingdom

saperebooks.com

ISBN: 978-1-913335-79-3

To the days of us

ACKNOWLEDGEMENTS

I thank Lovat Dickson and Teresa Sacco for suggesting, some years ago, that I should write about my Lancashire background; Adrian Leaman for his eloquence on social geography, and recommended reading; Leon Drucker for hunting down an 1829 edition of *Horse-Hoeing Husbandry* by Jethro Tull; Mr Walter Bennett, historian of Lancashire, for a long and invaluable letter full of information — and Miss Chris Simons, journalist, for introducing him to me; Mr J. R. Sutcliffe, General Secretary of the Lancashire Authors' Association; Mr Keith Bishop, County Archivist, and the Lancashire Record Office; the staff of Helston Branch Library, Cornwall, for obtaining books with such interest and alacrity; Felix, for listening to, commenting upon, and living with the Howarths, past, present, and to come; finally to my forebears and their circle, who seemed to come forward in a great host when I began to write this book, saying 'Remember us?' — I did, I do, and I shall.

J.S.

COURTING

ONE

A man sat penning his future, by candlelight. In the thirty-fifth year of life, he was trying to express something of great importance to a woman and a world little known to him, though she had become such a familiar part of his inner self that he could hardly think her an acquaintance. He was offering all he possessed, which might mean little to her but much to him and had been sufficient until he met her.

Inside, the fire on the broad hearth, and two sleeping dogs, kept him company. Outside, the wind tuned up an orchestra of threatening sounds to which he did not respond, for his farmhouse had been built into the side of the hill, with stone quarried from its heart, and would withstand centuries of tempest. Time was of small consequence here, and life was simple. A man woke with the coming of day, and stopped work at twilight. When he was hungry or thirsty, he ate and drank. When he was tired, he slept. And when he loved, as Ned Howarth did, he wrote his lady a letter and hoped to begin a new dynasty.

Kit's Hill,
Nick o' Garth,
Lancashire
Martinmas, 11 November 1760

Dear Lady Miss,
Happen you remember me. I am Ned Howarth the farmer that raises his hat to you every Market Day this three year past and once I had the Honour of taking your Arm and helping you and your Lady Aunt out of

the Crush at Preston Fair and we have spoke about my Horse and the Weather and All.

My dear Mother as died just afore Harvesting this Year used to say as Folk was wed to the Place they was born in and thats how I am with Kits Hill. They say as theres been a Howarth farming Kits Hill since the Hill were there but I wouldnt Swear on Holy Book to the Truth of that though I Feel it in my Bones. Dear Miss since Father died and the Sisters was wed and left Home and Brother Will went to Sea and was Drownded and Mother Took Poorly along of all the Fret, Dear Miss, Kits Hill and me has Lost Heart as you might say. Betty Ackroyd do the Cooking and Hens and Dairywork and the little lass Nellie do the Cleaning and Martha Glegg comes up from Garth on Washday but it seems Poor Sort o Work compared to what it might be Which not meaning to Offend is the Point Im coming at.

Dear Lady Miss Im not Rich but Im not Poor neither and Kits Hill is a Grand Place and theres Plenty to Eat and a Laugh or two round the Fire of an Evening. I know that your Aunt is a Kind Lady but wouldnt you rather live in Your Own House instead of Hers and have the Ordering of Us? I know your not used to Farming Ways but your very Quick and Smart at Learning and you could fetch your Bits and Pieces with you and have a little Parlour if You didnt want to Sit in the Kitchen and do your Stitching and Read your Book and youd be so Welcome dear Miss. Dear Miss I know You are of Age though You dont look it Else I would have wrote to your Aunt but then She might have seen me Off. So I am Asking if You would do me the Honour to be My Wife and if You dont want me then I ask your Pardon meaning no Offence but we have spoke so Friendly like these Three Year Past and I should be Honoured if You and your Lady Aunt Call on me Any Day and Betty Ackroyd is a Grand Baker Else I will be Honoured to Call on You if that is more Proper but perhaps youd let me know One Way or Tother as soon as Convenient for I think the World of You Miss I do.

Your Humble Servant, Ned Howarth.

9

Dear Mr Howarth

I am very Sensible of the Honour you do me, and Grateful for the many Kindnesses shewn me, and since I received your Letter yesterday, I have Pondered and Prayed that I might make the Right Decision and so not Wrong us both. You are Too Good to trust to my Abilities without Proof of their Worth, and I fear you might soon Tire of my ignorance in such Matters as are Naturally Incumbent upon her who is Mistress of Kit's Hill. I might Fail you, sir, and in so failing fail Myself, for I have some few Accomplishments of a Different Sort. Is it not Strange (all being Equal in the sight of God) that in this World we are Trained Up to Inequalities of every Kind? I could Commend myself into your Safekeeping, yet would I Hesitate to Recommend myself as your Wife…

On the title of *Wife*, her pen paused. So far, so fair, she thought. But Dorcas Wilde could be independent only in spirit, and a future rested on her present judgement. If she left the known custody of her aunt, she must accept the unknown custody of a husband. Whichever way the trap opened, she reflected, it would shut again.

'So that it does not close upon my fingers!' she remarked, and laid down her pen and chafed her hands together, for the room was cold despite a fire in the grate.

Then she read his letter again, with a smile for its homely phrasing, a delicate knitting of the brows for its spelling, and something softer of expression for the man himself. She had been guilty of charming Ned Howarth but not of soliciting this proposal. They were too unlike for matching, and he knew that and had yet been brave enough to broach the matter. She folded the letter carefully and slipped it in her pocket, where it reminded her by every shift and rustle of its presence that she was loved and wanted. She walked over to her bedroom window and leaned against the shutter, looking down into the street.

Her face was not vapid enough to be called pretty, for Dorcas was encumbered with intelligence and the Wildes' strong features. Her nose was slightly aquiline, her mouth decisive, her narrow eyes dark and brilliant; but a discerning person could take pleasure in watching her changes of expression. A smile would dissolve the severity, anger increase its haughty aspect, tranquillity reveal its peculiar beauty. She would grow handsomer with age, exchanging her present graceful carriage for a straighter back and a head held higher. She wore her own black hair, unpowdered and simply dressed. Her demeanour was modest, her voice soft, her wit sharp: a strange woman to catch a farmer's fancy, for he was as open and frank as a summer's day while Dorcas was all night.

One would have imagined that Ned Howarth's easy body, his wheat-gold head and good blue eyes, were better suited to a simple wench — though there was a warmth within and about him that attracted most women, and had drawn even the self-contained Miss Dorcas Wilde to exchange good-days. He was of the earth, yet as gentle as any gentleman should be and more chivalrous than many. A man whose mouth was tender, whose smile was unrestrained, who gave every appetite its due and was not ridden by any. In anger he grew red, and shouted, but his temper was quick and fair and soon forgiven. *Happen you remember me.* Oh, she remembered him with affection, glad that such men existed (though not for her, they were so very different). Musing in the white light of a winter afternoon, Dorcas knew what her reply should be.

For the old market town of Millbridge was a handsome example of man's progress in the art of subduing nature. The churches took care of his soul, the shops his daily needs, the houses his shelter, the inns his pleasure, the grammar school his education, and the poor his service. Above the town stood Kersall Park, rebuilt in 1655, to rouse his worldly reverence and cause him to doff his hat on Sundays as the Kersalls filed into their family pew. Millbridge was awake and thriving, conscious of its historical and economic importance in the valley. Its Fair charter had been granted in 1589, and every second Monday from Easter to Christmas the drovers came with their herds from miles around. In addition, there was a weekly market on Saturdays where you could see as much as £5,000 change hands in as little as an hour. Here, huckaback table linen from the Preston area was sold, stout dimity for bedroom hangings from Manchester, fustians from Blackburn, woollens and worsted cloth from Bury. Farmers' wives drove in to sell their butter and eggs and cheese. There was a Hiring Fair where servants might be purchased for a season or a lifetime. Millbridge was as compact, as busy, and as rich as a hive, while her prosperity increased.

Looking down the High Street, Dorcas could see the crossroads where Middletown Street (once the Roman Way) ran at right angles. Beyond this junction lay the new corn market and Lower Gate, which eventually gave access to the new turnpike road running from Keighley to Kendal. Turning her head to the left she had a view of the market square, dominated by a coaching inn at the far end. This hostelry, for fifty years The Royal Oak, was re-named The Royal George when the first Hanoverian king ascended the English throne. Now the third monarch of that title was in the first year of his reign, and the landlord had mounted a new florid-faced and bewigged sign to show that he moved with the times. (But The Red Lion, a farmers' tavern at the back of the square, remained true to John of Gaunt's ancient symbol.) The spire of St

Mark's church dominated the skyline, with the rectory chimneys just visible below it and smoking frugally on the frosty air. And had Dorcas chosen her bedroom at the back of Thornton House, instead of the front, she would have seen the long garden going down to the banks of the River Wynden, and had a fine view of the corn mill and the pack-horse bridge (which together had given the town its name). Within the last three decades, the spinners and weavers had been allowed to ply their crafts in the row of cottages further downstream, and on summer evenings the sound of shuttle and wheel came faintly upon the ear. While, out of sight of gentlefolk, was a fulling mill and a dye-house; and well away from their noses, tanners and leather-workers plied their trades. A place for everyone, and everyone in his place, the Reverend Walter Jarrett always said, implying that the social order should not change — except, of course, in heaven, where it would instantly be reversed.

Here Dorcas Wilde had lived as companion to her Aunt Tabitha for three quiescent years, following the death of both parents. The air was harsher, the land poorer than in her father's Gloucestershire parish, but genteel existence was much the same. A cup of chocolate at eight, dinner at one o'clock, tea-drinking between four and five, and a substantial supper at seven. Between mealtimes, a lady could study her book, ply her needle, take an airing if the weather were fine, and admire or deplore her face in the glass. Sometimes there was a musical evening, or a modest assembly with dancing and refreshment. Otherwise, Dorcas played backgammon or piquet with her aunt, lit her candle, said her prayers, and retired to her bed.

...but wouldnt you rather live in Your Own House instead of Hers and have the Ordering of Us?

Along the Wyndendale Valley, with its muddy chain of villages and hamlets, life wore a different aspect. Here rose the Pennines in desolate majesty, where the wind ruled, and ways were steep enough to make a horse uneasy, and snow might trap the unwary traveller or some black precipice await his careless step. Swarth Moor, Bleak Low, Th'Stoops, Nick o' Garth.

Single files of flagstones criss-crossing the moors marked pack-horse tracks, where caravans of woolmen had trodden and driven their loads from scattered farmsteads to the clothing centres for centuries. Drovers had beaten out their wider way, grass-verged and worn by the passage of time and man and beast, which cut through from Yorkshire by Scarth Nick, and wandered down the dale to proud Preston which held the finest of fairs. While up on Garth Fells, out of the cosy bustle of village life and close neighbours, a handful of old farms raised stone walls against the elements and defied them. Their sheep and cattle were leaner than those in the valley, their crops less sweet and plentiful, their people hardier and more steadfast. These random fortresses, strategically placed in the war against nature, bore names that flew like pennons in the prevailing wind. Long Hay, Foxholes, Shap Fold, Windygate, Kit's Hill. Kit's Hill. Spring came slowly here, with small cold flowers. Summer had hardly warmed the heather and cotton grass before autumn fetched down the leaves. Then winter closed its hands upon them.

I know your not used to Farming Ways but your very Quick and Smart at Learning...

Another life, another world, Dorcas mused. Her woollen gown smouldered rich and green against the painted shutter. Her face was ivory in the failing light. She was so sheltered, so motionless.

Phoebe Jarrett, the rector's daughter, appeared at the junction between Rectory Lane and the Market Square, wearing a mantle with a beaver-lined hood and beaver trimming, and experiencing some difficulty with her pattens.

'Does one wear a mantle and hood at Kit's Hill?' Dorcas asked herself, watching Miss Jarrett's teetering progress down the High Street.

She supposed not, for the wind would snatch at fashion. Farmers' wives wore coarse white caps and shawls, or strapped old bonnets onto their heads as though they were helmets to be worn against the foe. Farmers' wives had red hands and faces, chapped by the wind, and their clothes were meant to warm them rather than to set off to advantage a trim waist and a neat ankle.

'Not even a ribbon to grace them!' Dorcas remarked aloud, and rapped the bedroom windowpane with her knuckles to attract Miss Jarrett's attention. For they were both daughters of the Church, both spinsters in their anxious twenties, and friends of a shy and trusting sort. On an impulse, Dorcas threw up the sash window and called down softly into the High Street.

'Phoebe! Phoebe!' Making a pantomime of the fact that she wanted to speak to her privately, and they must not disturb Miss Wilde, who snored with her dog in the parlour below.

But even as she pattered downstairs and opened the front door herself, the voice of her aunt sounded the alarm.

'Agnes! Dorcas! What's amiss? Who's there? Why have you not told me? Agnes! Where's Agnes?' Who was this moment appearing from the kitchen at the end of the long hall, wiping competent hands on a clean apron. 'Agnes!'

Then she rang her handbell incessantly, and the spaniel Walpole began to bark and growl and make little runs at the parlour door, to show that he knew a burglar when he heard one.

'Oh, mercy on us!' said Dorcas drily, 'you would think I had been fetched home by the Constable. I so wished to speak with you privately, but now you must come and show my aunt your new mantle.'

Miss Jarrett would not marry now. Her father had needed her too long. Her future was assured until he died, and would then become a terrifying question for a faded gentlewoman to answer.

Dear Lady Miss Im not Rich but Im not Poor neither...

Dorcas cried, 'Come in out of the cold, Phoebe!' And over her shoulder said to the servant Agnes, 'It is Miss Jarrett, and she will take tea with us, so put on the kettle if you please!'

Then beguiled her custodian by popping her head round the parlour door, saying, 'Look who has called to show us her new mantle, Aunt Tib!' Giving Walpole a little nudge with the toe of her slipper to silence him.

'Ah, now I see,' said Miss Wilde, setting down the handbell at last. 'Well, Miss Jarrett, Dorcas has been sulking in her room since dinner, so I hope you will instruct her better with regard to her duty. Sit there, where I can see you. Why have you bought such a garment? I hope it did not cost too much. Is it come from Manchester?'

It was quite beautiful, Dorcas reflected, to watch Phoebe bring this little bedlam to order. She inquired after Miss Wilde's health with a concentrated frown of concern, though the old lady would possibly outlive them all. She patted Walpole until he ceased trying to bully her. She settled her hoop and skirts and herself onto a prim chair, and assured her questioner that the mantle was a gift, not new at all, and exceedingly warm to wear. So Miss Wilde, cheated of this victim, turned upon her niece instead.

'Well, Miss, have you wrote your refusal?' And, before Dorcas could answer her, gave Phoebe an explanation. 'I should not like this noised abroad, Miss Jarrett, but some impudent jackanapes of a labourer has tried to make away with my money.'

'Indeed, ma'am?' said Phoebe, bewildered.

'Since you vowed me to silence on the matter, ma'am,' cried Dorcas, indignant, 'I should not have expected you to mention it.'

'I do as I please, miss, in my own house.'

'So I observe, ma'am, and wish that I were able to follow your example.'

'That you cannot, without you having your own money, miss.'

'Oh, ma'am. Oh, Dorcas.'

Then Agnes came in, carrying the second-best china on a silver tray, and the ladies had to speak of other matters until she had gone.

'I think only of your good, miss,' said her aunt, lifting the silver teapot.

Dorcas did not answer her, but turned to Phoebe, saying, 'This was the very matter on which I had hoped to consult you privately.'

'There is no need of privacy and consultation, miss. Tell the blockhead to go about his business, and get him a serving-wench if he feels so inclined.'

Dorcas again addressed her friend, while Walpole begged for a biscuit.

'I have this day received a — proposal — a proposal of marriage. From Mr Edward Howarth of Kit's Hill. You know how we have often spoke with him, and he is something of a favourite with your father. I believe his offer — though mistaken, though unexpected — to be genuine. But my aunt insists that he has designs on her property, through me!'

'The rascal knows very well,' said Miss Wilde, feeding Walpole and making a slop in the saucers, 'that all this will be left to Dorcas when I am gone, and so he makes the chit an offer.'

All this. The tall house and long garden, linen on high shelves and clothes in deep closets, old-fashioned jewellery in locked boxes, chiming clocks in silent rooms. All this, which Miss Wilde could not take with her at the last, but would if she could, and clutter heaven.

Phoebe was smoothing her muff, head bent. When she did speak, she had marshalled her few facts.

'But Mr Edward Howarth is a most gentlemanlike fellow, ma'am. Though not, of course, what one would expect for Dorcas. I know him pretty well by repute, and folk think highly of him. He is quiet-spoken and honest, and somewhat independent in nature and manner. I cannot believe he has designs of the sort you mention. Why, ma'am, did he not assist you from Preston Fair when you was took faint?'

'Aye, so he did,' cried Miss Wilde, vindicated, 'and now I am sure I felt his hand upon my purse. Did I not say so at the time, Dorcas?'

'No, ma'am, you did not. You said you was very grateful to Mr Howarth and wished we might receive him, but that would not be proper.'

'Besides, ma'am,' Phoebe said firmly, for between Miss Wilde's obstinacy and Dorcas's persistence there was hardly room to speak, 'you are like to live many more years yet, please God, and you can always change your Will.'

Miss Wilde shook a silver spoon at her caller, for emphasis.

'Mark my words, Miss Jarrett. If Dorcas was to take this villain, I should be burned in my bed!'

'Oh, fiddle!' said Dorcas.

'I do not follow your reasoning, ma'am,' said Phoebe, accepting a slopped cup of tea and a sugar biscuit.

But there was no reasoning to follow.

'He is beneath her entirely,' Miss Wilde continued, as though no one had spoken. 'A paltry fellow with his dunghill farm and his sheep and pigs and poultry. Why, what should Dorcas do there, pray? She has Greek and Latin, as well as the usual accomplishments. For her father (my brother Ambrose) having no son to teach, taught his daughter instead. So she is no use to herself or any husband. Neither fish, flesh, nor good red herring!'

Having thus dismissed three people at a blow, Miss Wilde contented herself with sipping tea and persuading Walpole to catch pieces of biscuit.

'I should be obliged if you would read Mr Howarth's letter, Phoebe,' said Dorcas. Not without a twinge for its lack of polish.

Which her friend did, and handed it back with a little smile.

'There is nothing but proper respect and proper feeling in this proposal, ma'am,' said Phoebe, addressing Miss Wilde, 'and Mr Howarth deserves no less from anyone that reads it. You may be assured that I shall not mention this matter — no, not even to my father, if that is your wish.'

She declined further refreshment, and made her apologies and farewells. Dorcas followed her into the hall pensively, and held her muff while she strapped on her pattens.

'But what shall I say to him?' Dorcas asked.

'I have had no experience of such matters. I presume you thank him for the honour, and decline as graciously as may be, with the hope that some other lady more worthy than yourself will make him happy. Yes, that should do very well.'

She was in quite a fluster with her gloves, imagining rejected lovers.

'And if I decline him, Phoebe, what then?'

'*If* you decline him? Surely you cannot contemplate… What then, you say? What would Miss Wilde do without you?'

'She would doubtless find some other female companion to humiliate.'

'You are disturbed, as is natural, and do not know what you say.'

'I am disturbed, certainly, but mean every word of it! Well, do not entirely hate me. I shall need a friend. Do you not like Mr Howarth?'

'Who could not like him? Aye, and esteem him?'

'And yet he is not good enough to be married?'

'Not to you, I think.' Firmly.

'But do you understand me when I say that in this letter, and in his presence too — what little conversation I have had with him — there is a warmth and kindliness to which a woman could respond?'

'It would not do for a lady, Dorcas.' Very firmly.

'Too poor to be married to a gentleman, and too fine to be married to a yeoman farmer! Oh, if only I had money I should not need to marry at all!'

'Do not think me indelicate or overbearing,' Phoebe whispered from beneath the beaver-lined hood, 'but I should have liked to marry, whether I had money or no. A clerical gentleman, such as my father. And I should so have cared for him and his parish and (do not think me forward!) for his children. Yes, indeed I should, and have been blessed. But I am very fortunate. Do not imagine that I complain!'

From the sepulchre of the hall Agnes asked, 'Should I light the candles now, miss?'

'Yes, if you please,' cried Dorcas, but Phoebe had not quite done with good advice.

Homely and sturdy in her second-hand mantle, the vision of the clerical gentleman fading before the reality of her walk home, she endeavoured to soften their spinsterhood.

'Better to enjoy a single blessedness,' she whispered, 'than the discontent that must attend an unequal match.'

Dear Miss I know You are of Age though You dont look it…

Dorcas embraced her friend gently, and closed the door upon her unassuming back.

'I will take a candlestick up with me, Agnes, before supper. For I have a letter to finish.'

…and yet I hesitate to Recommend myself as your Wife.

She had sat an hour before the page. Now her pen darted at the final sentences.

Sir, I am forced to speak plain, and trust you will not regard my Honesty as Immodesty. I have but Twenty Pound a Year of my Own, which was my Mother's, and some few Pretty Things that belonged to her. The Rest was all Sold Up, for my Father was a Man of God that Practised what he Preached, and so Diminished his Substance. I have no other Expectations. If you have heard Differently, you are Mistook.

A True Wife should possess the Necessary Qualities to act as her Husband's Companion throughout Life, and some Fortune with which to Endow him. I should but Burthen you, sir.

If this Answer should cause you some Distress, pray you Forgive Her who is the Unwilling Cause of it. God Bless and Keep you, Sir.

Yours, Dorcas Wilde

Kit's Hill,
Nick o' Garth,
Lancashire

15 November 1790

Dear Lady Madam Wilde,
I believe I should have Wrote to You First and I Humbly ask your
Pardon if I did wrong. Madam Lady I wish to have the Honour of your
Lady Niece's Hand in Marriage which the Lady Miss Dorcas has Told
me is no Use since She has no Fortune nor Expecting None. I have
Enough for Both and I am not asking your Lady Niece to Work as I
have a mort of Servants and She shall live here as Fine as Fi'pence at
Kits Hill and only have the Ordering of Us and be Genteel and
Comfortable. If you would do me the Honour to See me and let me
explain I could make us all Easy and dear Lady Madam you would be
Welcome at Kits Hill as a Queen when you wanted and I could send Tom
to Millbridge to Fetch you in the Dogcart.
Your Humble Servant, Ned Howarth.

'Is the numskull entirely mad?' cried Miss Wilde. 'Did you not
refuse him outright?'

'You know that I did,' replied Dorcas, very pale, very cold. 'I
understand this letter no more than you do yourself, ma'am. It
would seem that his regard for me is greater than his desire to
make off with your property!'

'You had best watch your tongue, miss, or you and I will part
company. So he would make me easy in mind, would he? And
send Tom with the dog-cart when I wanted to visit? Why,
miss, this country lover of yours is a proper wag! Were I
accustomed to entertain labourers in my parlour, I might send
for him to keep us company. We grow dull together of an